Diego Saves a Butterfly

adapted by Lara Bergen
based on the original teleplay by Madellaine Paxson
illustrated by Warner McGee

SCHOLASTIC INC.
New York Toronto London Auckland Sydney
Mexico City New Delhi Hong Kong Buenos Aires

Hi! I am .
DIEGO

Look at this !
COCOON

Do you know what is inside?

It is a  !

It is a Blue Morpho !

"Let me see!" says  .
BABY JAGUAR

Oh, no!

The ![butterfly] flew away.
BUTTERFLY

I think ![baby jaguar]
BABY JAGUAR

scared the ![butterfly] .
BUTTERFLY

Do not worry,  .
BABY JAGUAR

CLICK can help us

find the .
BUTTERFLY

Just say "📷"!

CLICK

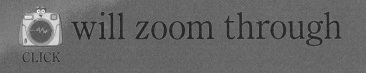 will zoom through

the rainforest to look for

the .

BUTTERFLY

Is this the ?

BUTTERFLY

No, this is a .

LADYBUG

Is this the ?

BUTTERFLY

Yes!

BUTTERFLIES live

in the rainforest.

But this **BUTTERFLY**

is in a **CAVE**.

The **CAVE** is cold!

We have to bring the **BUTTERFLY**

back to the warm rainforest.

Come on!

Now we are in the 🕳️.
CAVE

But the 🕳️ is so dark!
CAVE

🎒 can help us see.
RESCUE PACK

Here is  !
RESCUE PACK

Can  help us see?

No.

Can a  help us see?
FLASHLIGHT

Yes!

There is the !
BUTTERFLY

"I am too cold to fly," says the 🦋 BUTTERFLY.

That is okay, 🦋 BUTTERFLY.

You can ride with me.

BUTTERFLIES like to sip juice from **FRUIT** .

Do you see any ?

FRUIT

"Yum!" says the  .
BUTTERFLY

The 🥔 was good.
FRUIT

The  is warm
BUTTERFLY

again.

Now she can fly!

To the rainforest!

Come on!

Oh, no!

There is a big  !
BIRD

The  is afraid of  .
BUTTERFLY   BIRDS

When the  opens its wings, the BIRD flies away. The BUTTERFLY is brave!

We made it back
to the rainforest.
But where is  ?
BABY JAGUAR

"Here I am," says  BABY JAGUAR.

"I do not want to scare the BUTTERFLY.

I want to be friends."

"Me too!" says the BUTTERFLY.

Thanks for helping us save the  !

BUTTERFLY

And thanks for helping

BABY JAGUAR

make a new friend too!